# BOND
## GIRLS

# BOND
## GIRLS

**Alastair Dougall**

# CONTENTS

# Dr. No ™

**Murder and radioactive rocks** lead Bond to investigate
the mysterious Dr. No. Bond lands on Dr. No's private
Caribbean island expecting danger. Instead he
encounters seashell collector Honey Ryder. Beautiful,
confident, and fearless, Honey is a woman who knows
how to take care of herself. Bond has no choice but to
involve her in his efforts to foil Dr. No's plan to "topple"
American rockets. He makes sure she gets out alive when
Dr. No's base finally goes into meltdown.

What's your name?
**Ryder.**
Ryder what?
**Honey Ryder.**

Bond and **Honey**

# HONEY RYDER

**The knife** that hung from Honey's bikini belt was not just for show. It was useful for collecting valuable shells. It was also useful in case of any trouble. The handsome stranger, James Bond, seemed harmless, but Honey wasn't taking any chances. If he wasn't looking for shells, what was he doing on Crab Key, Dr. No's island?

**As Dr. No's guards** scoured the island, Bond convinced Honey that they were in danger on the beach. She agreed to hide with Bond and his friend Quarrel.

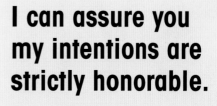

**I can assure you my intentions are strictly honorable.**

Bond to Honey Ryder

# SYLVIA

**She liked excitement** and James Bond, the man she had just met at Le Cercle's chemin de fer tables, promised just that. What a pity he had been called away. Losing had made Sylvia Trench feel reckless. She felt like taking one more gamble. She had Bond's card. Why wait?

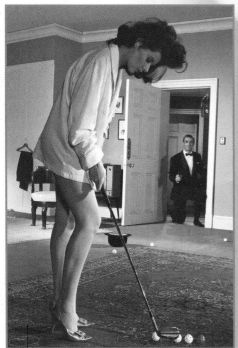

**In the small hours,** Bond returned home from MI6 to find an elegant intruder with a liking for golf wearing his pyjama top.

Too bad you have to go. Just as things were getting interesting.

Sylvia Trench to Bond

# Miss
# MONEYPENNY

**Seated at her desk** outside of M's office at MI6's headquarters, Miss Moneypenny sometimes speculated about the secret service personnel that visited her irascible but good-hearted boss. She had a soft spot for one in particular: Double-O-Seven, James Bond. As well as being extremely efficient, Miss Moneypenny had a good sense of humor and loved to flirt with MI6's most charismatic agent. She sometimes wondered where flirting with him could lead…

## What gives?
Me—given an ounce of encouragement.

**Bond** and Miss Moneypenny

**I'll just go and put some clothes on.**
Don't go to any trouble on my account.

**Miss Taro** and Bond

# MISS TARO

**She was surprised** to see James Bond. That was putting it mildly. Miss Taro, a secretary at Government House in Kingston, Jamaica, and a spy for Dr. No, had been informed that Bond would be eliminated on the twisting mountain road leading to her house. The telephone rang. In hushed tones so that Bond would not hear, Miss Taro agreed to keep him there for a couple of hours. That was not difficult. Bond was in no hurry to leave. He realized he was being set up, but he was confident he had the situation under control.

**The seductive Miss Taro** gave Bond directions to her house. Assuming he would never arrive, she decided to take a bath.

# FROM RUSSIA WITH L♥VE ™

**A beautiful Russian corporal** in the KGB, Tatiana "Tania" Romanova, lures Bond to Istanbul. She claims to have fallen in love with Bond's photograph and wishes to defect to the West, bringing with her the Lektor, a top-secret Soviet decoder. Tania believes that she is on an important mission for her country's secret service, but she is the innocent dupe of an even more devious and ruthless organization, one with a special grudge against MI6 and Bond: SPECTRE.

You're one of the most beautiful girls I've ever seen. **Thank you, but I think my mouth is too big.** No—it's just the right size. For me, that is.

Bond and **Tania**

**Careful. Guns upset me.**
I'm sorry. I'm a bit upset myself!
**Tania** and Bond

# TATIANA ROMANOVA

**After an eventful evening,** Bond ordered breakfast for one from room service, ran a bath and got undressed. Then he heard a door shut. His bedroom door. Grabbing a towel and his gun, he crept onto the veranda and entered his bedroom through the french doors. A beguiling sight met his eyes. Tatiana "Tania" Romanova had begun the first part of her assignment.

**The attraction** was instant. Bond and Tania never suspected for a second that they were being filmed by SPECTRE agents.

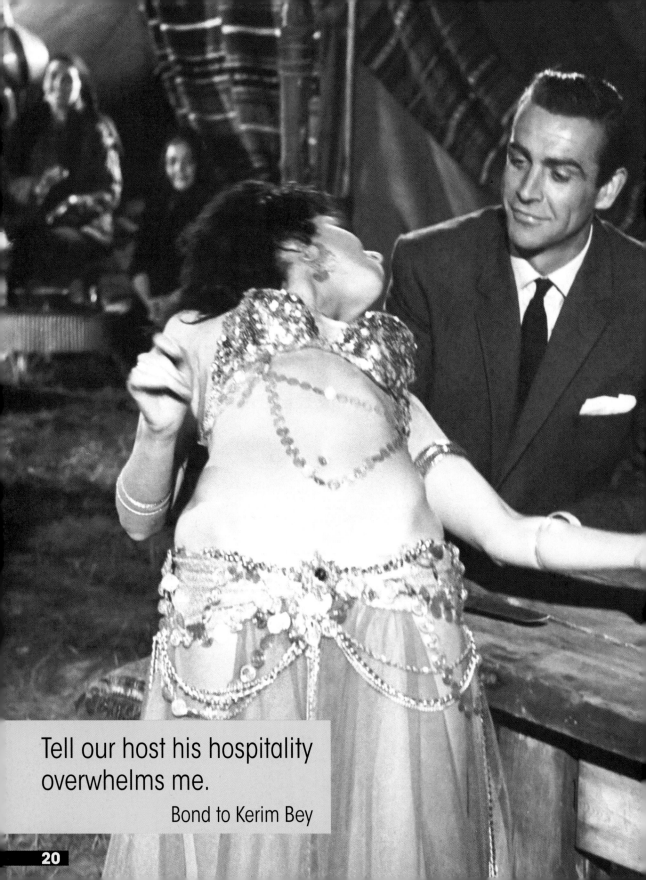

Tell our host his hospitality
overwhelms me.

Bond to Kerim Bey

# GYPSY CAMP

**"You'll like my gypsy friends."** Kerim Bey, Bond's Istanbul contact, decided that Bond needed protection from KGB assassin Krilencu and took him to a gypsy camp outside of the city. Bond appreciated belly dancer Leila, who ran through her full repertoire of moves. Then the entertainment took a more violent turn…

**Vida and Zora** loved the same man and fought to decide who deserved him. An attack by Krilencu stopped the fight.

# GOLDFINGER™

**Bond receives** a grim warning never to cross Auric Goldfinger again: a dead girl, Goldfinger's former companion Jill Masterson, painted gold from head to toe. M orders Bond to continue his investigation into the hugely wealthy Goldfinger, a suspected gold smuggler, but Bond gets too close. Captured by Goldfinger and his guards, Bond's only hope of escape is Pussy Galore, Goldfinger's voluptuous personal pilot. Somehow Bond must win Pussy over, persuade her to change sides, and help him to foil Operation Grand Slam, Goldfinger's master plan to destroy the gold reserve at Fort Knox with an atomic bomb.

## The girl's dead… and she's covered in paint. Gold paint.

Bond to Felix Leiter

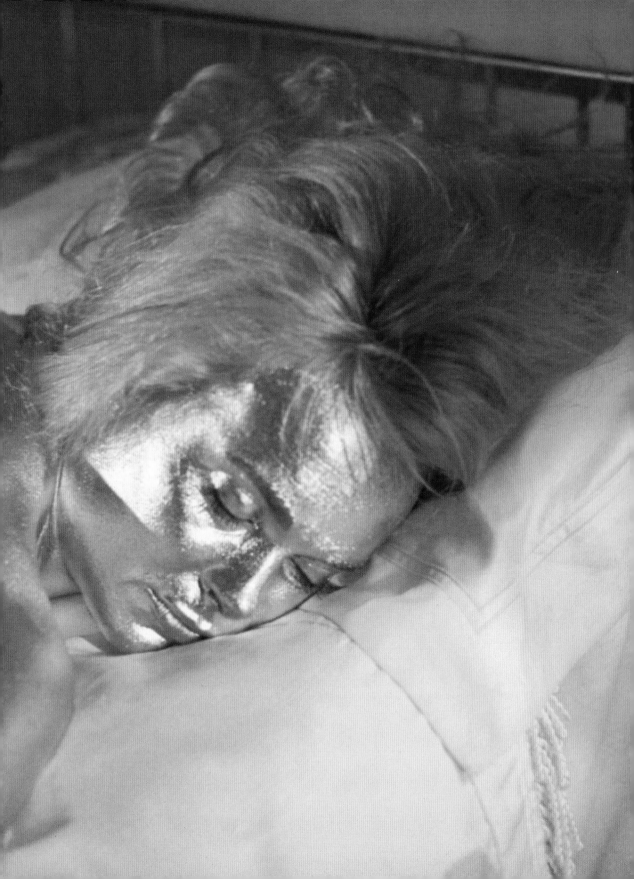

What would it take for you to see things my way?
**A lot more than you've got.**

Bond and **Pussy Galore**

# PUSSY GALORE

**The leader** of her own flying circus of female pilots, Pussy Galore was fiercely proud of her abilities—"I'm a damn good pilot"—and determined to resist Bond's teasing attempts to charm her. Yet, much to her annoyance, she couldn't help feeling attracted to the tall, dark, courageous spy, who showed no fear, despite being Goldfinger's prisoner.

**"You've asked for this"**—Pussy tried to put Bond in his place with a judo throw, but Bond had a few slick moves of his own.

# HAPPY LANDING

**They had foiled** Operation Grand Slam and saved the lives of thousands of American servicemen. They had evaded Goldfinger's final attempt to get revenge. They had survived a plane crash and Goldfinger was now "playing his golden harp." Concealed by parachute silk from prying eyes, Bond and Pussy seized the chance of a few moments together.

**No longer** on opposite sides, Bond and Pussy made a great team—it was Pussy who switched the gas in her planes' dispensers, ruining Goldfinger's murderous plot.

This is no time to be rescued...

Bond

# THUNDERBALL™

**SPECTRE hijacks** a NATO plane carrying two atomic bombs and holds Britain and the United States to ransom. Domino Derval, the missing pilot's sister, is the only lead. Bond travels to the Bahamas to find her. He discovers that she is involved with a man named Emilio Largo, a millionaire playboy twice her age who sports an eye patch and a SPECTRE signet ring.

It's the first time I've tasted women.
They're rather good.

Bond to Domino Derval

**You are not like Largo.**
Oh? Why do you say that?
**The way you… hold me.**

**Domino** and Bond

# DOMINO DERVAL

**Domino had met Largo** in Capri and been impressed by his wealth and urbanity. She was now finding life as Largo's mistress oppressive and innocently wondered if James Bond could be her escape route. Domino had some grim truths to discover: Bond was a British agent and Largo was a leading member of SPECTRE and responsible for her beloved brother's death.

**The atmosphere** of male rivalry when Largo invited Bond to lunch was not as harmless as Domino assumed.

# FIONA VOLPE

**Among the visitors** to Palmyra, Emilio Largo's magnificent estate, was SPECTRE assassin Fiona Volpe. Largo wanted Bond to be killed without delay, but Fiona believed that his death would attract unwanted attention to SPECTRE's grand plan. She preferred to eliminate Bond in her own special way: by seducing him first. Flame-haired Fiona Volpe of SPECTRE's Execution Branch would not be the first *femme fatale* to underestimate James Bond.

> When the time is right he will be killed… I shall kill him.
>
> Fiona Volpe to Emilio Largo

# PATRICIA FEARING

**A traction table** running out of control presented Patricia Fearing with a tricky problem. If Mr. Bond, who had nearly died, reported her, she might lose her job at Shrublands clinic. Pat was pretty sure he wouldn't say anything, but still… The price of Bond's silence was treatment of a very different kind. It was a price Pat didn't really mind paying at all.

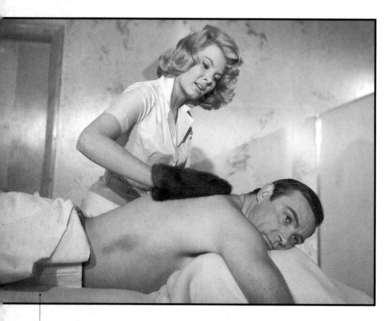

**Bond** had checked into the clinic for rest and recuperation. Patricia Fearing and a possible SPECTRE plot ensured that his visit was full of incident.

Do I seem healthy?
**Too healthy by far.**
Bond and **Patricia Fearing**

# YOU ONLY LIVE TWICE

**M sends Bond to Japan** to investigate the hijacking of an American spacecraft. Bond experiences a new way of life, learns ninja techniques, and even takes a Japanese bride. While battling SPECTRE's plot to start a third world war, Bond gets to know Aki and Kissy, two of the Japanese Secret Service's most attractive and resourceful agents.

**I love you.** I have a car nearby. **Oh? Where do you suggest we go.** I know a quiet hotel. **And?** Where your friend is waiting: Mr. Henderson.

**Bond** and Aki

# KISSY

**In order to search** the island of Matsu for the enemy's base, Bond needed the perfect cover. Tiger Tanaka, head of the Japanese Secret Service, disguised Bond as a local Ama fisherman and even provided him with an Ama bride. Her name was Kissy Suzuki and she was one of Tanaka's finest agents.

**Kissy was** a superb swimmer and an excellent shot. These skills proved vital when she and Bond discovered SPECTRE's rocket base, hidden inside a dormant volcano.

# Some honeymoon…

Bond to Kissy

I think I will very much
enjoy serving under you.

Aki to Bond

# AKI

**"I love you."** The password M and Miss Moneypenny had given Bond was certainly easy to remember. And when Bond made contact with charming Japanese secret agent Aki, it also seemed appropriate: Aki would certainly be easy to fall in love with. Later, gunmen employed by SPECTRE closed in, and Bond had good reason to be thankful for quick-thinking Aki and her Toyota sports car.

**Bond and Aki's** relationship proved tragically short-lived: she was poisoned by a SPECTRE assassin.

# ON HER MAJESTY'S
# SECRET SERVICE ™

**While hunting** Ernst Stavro Blofeld, Bond saves tempestuous Teresa "Tracy" Di Vicenzo from drowning herself. Tracy's father, underworld boss Marc Ange Draco, offers to tell Bond where Blofeld is if Bond will marry his rebellious daughter. But before that can happen, Bond must infiltrate Blofeld's latest operation: an allergy clinic where the only patients are Angels of Death—beautiful girls from all over the world.

I love you. I know I'll never find another girl like you.
Will you marry me? **You mean it?** I mean it.

Bond and **Tracy**

**Suppose I were to kill you for a thrill.**
I can think of something more sensible to do.

**Tracy** and Bond

# TRACY DI VICENZO

**Her real name** was Teresa but, as she told Bond, "Teresa was a saint. I'm known as Tracy." Bond had saved her from suicide and bailed her out at the casino. Tracy prided herself on always paying off her debts, so she simply left Bond her hotel room key. But that was too obvious. Tracy prided herself on being wild, reckless, unpredictable. She would surprise Bond and wait in *his* room.

**"Why do you persist** in rescuing me, Mr. Bond?" asked Tracy. Bond admitted it was becoming a habit.

# ANGELS OF DEATH

**The female patients** at Piz Gloria, the clinic run by the "Comte de Bleuchamp," were bored. The sight of Bond in a kilt provided a welcome distraction. Of course, nothing was as it seemed: "Bleuchamp" was Blofeld; Bond was an imposter; and the girls were unwitting Angels of Death.

I'm afraid I've never had much to do with ladies.

Bond as Sir Hilary Bray

# Diamonds Are Forever™
## Forever
## Forever

**After avenging** Tracy's murder by killing Blofeld, Bond infiltrates a diamond-smuggling pipeline and encounters the alluring Tiffany Case. She's not concerned about right and wrong—she's just interested in diamonds. Bond eventually convinces Tiffany to side with him against his old enemy, Ernst Stavro Blofeld—back from the dead with a new face and a diamond-encrusted superweapon with which to threaten the world.

That's quite a nice little nothing you're almost wearing. I approve. **I don't dress for the hired help.**

Bond and **Tiffany Case**

## I never mix business with pleasure.

Tiffany to Bond

# TIFFANY CASE

**"You're not a cop** and you're not Peter Franks!" Tiffany was no fool. Bond had tricked her into believing he was Franks, a link in the diamond-smuggling pipeline. Now the smugglers were being killed off, and she was next. Tiffany opted to play ball with Bond and the CIA against the man behind the smuggling ring: Ernst Stavro Blofeld. Now, if only she could get those diamonds…

**On board** Blofeld's oil-rig base, Tiffany pretended to go along with his plan to use a diamond satellite weapon to hold the world to ransom.

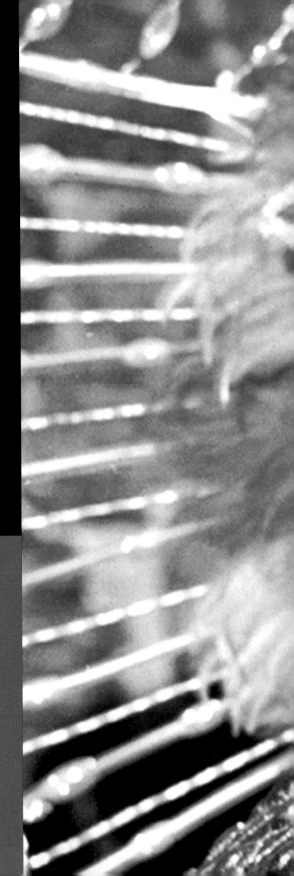

# LIVE AND LET DIE ™

**Solitaire,** a beautiful, innocent fortune-teller, unwittingly holds the key to a conspiracy to flood the US with cheap heroin. The plot's mastermind, Dr. Kananga, relies on Solitaire's telepathic powers and tarot cards to keep one step ahead of the authorities. Bond senses that if he can win Solitaire over, he can send Kananga's vicious, voodoo-driven empire straight to the graveyard.

A man comes. He travels quickly. He has purpose. He comes over water. He travels with others. He will oppose. He brings violence and destruction.

Solitaire foresees Bond's arrival

# SOLITAIRE

**The cards decreed** that she and Bond would be lovers. As Kananga berated Solitaire for her "impertinence," she could feel herself drifting toward Bond and away from Kananga, alienated by his threats. She felt powerless to resist her fate and, truth to tell, she had no wish to.

Your power exists to serve me. And it is mine to control. If and when the time comes I decide you are to lose it, I myself will take it away.

Kananga to Solitaire

## Mrs. Bond,
## I presume?

Bond to Rosie

# ROSIE CARVER

**Bond was her second assignment.** Rosie's first had resulted in a dead British agent, so Bond was naturally cautious about this CIA operative, who had checked in as "Mrs. Bond." Bond believed that Rosie was well-meaning, if easily scared by voodoo charms. Then he received a tip-off—a tarot card. It implied that Rosie could not be trusted.

**Bond and Rosie** traveled to San Monique, Kananga's island. Suspecting Rosie was a double agent, Bond was determined to discover what she knew.

# THE MAN WITH THE GOLDEN GUN ™

**The gold bullet** inscribed "007" sends a clear message. Scaramanga, The Man With the Golden Gun, the world's most notorious assassin, is hunting MI6's top agent. Bond goes looking for the mysterious killer and, with help from Agent Mary Goodnight, tracks down Scaramanga's lover, Andrea Anders. Unknown to Bond, Andrea has her own agenda: she longs to be free of Scaramanga and his cruelty. Scaramanga, meanwhile, is more concerned about getting hold of the Solex Agitator, a top-secret solar-energy device, than with Bond. At least for the time being.

He's a monster—I hate him.
**Then leave him.**
You don't walk out on Scaramanga.

Andrea Anders and **Bond**

# You always take a shower with a pistol?

Bond to Andrea

# ANDREA ANDERS

**Bond had anticipated** a cool reception. He had not expected that Andrea Anders would come out of the shower holding a gun. Fortunately, it only took a little arm-twisting to get her to reveal Scaramanga's next appointment: at the Bottoms Up club. Bond never suspected that Andrea was praying he would kill Scaramanga.

**"Bottoms up!"** Bond and Andrea toasted their uneasy pact with champagne, which Bond had thoughtfully brought with him.

There's more to you than meets the eye, Goodnight.

Bond

# GOODNIGHT

**Agent Goodnight** knew that things had not gone well. Instead of obtaining the Solex Agitator for Bond, she had allowed master assassin Scaramanga to kidnap her and take the Solex for himself. A prisoner on Scaramanga's island, Goodnight promised herself to do her bravest and best when Bond came to rescue her.

**While Bond** and Scaramanga dueled , Goodnight knocked out the mechanic at Scaramanga's solar energy plant—and started an explosive chain reaction.

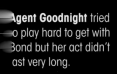

**Agent Goodnight** tried to play hard to get with Bond but her act didn't last very long.

# THE SPY WHO LOVED ME™

**Major Anya Amasova,** Agent Triple X, has never failed on a mission.
Neither has James Bond. After competing to obtain secret microfilm
of a submarine tracking system, Bond and Anya join together in an
unprecedented alliance between MI6 and the KGB. Their objective is
to investigate shipping magnate Karl Stromberg, suspected of
hijacking a British and a Soviet nuclear sub. After narrowly escaping
death with Bond on several occasions, Anya discovers that on a
previous assignment Bond killed her KGB lover. She promises Bond
her lover's death will not go unavenged.

## When this mission is over – I will kill you.

**Anya Amasova** to Bond

# ANYA AMASOVA

**The mission is over, Commander.**

Anya Amasova

**The time had come.** Karl Stromberg's plan to cause nuclear Armageddon and rule what was left of the world from his undersea empire had been thwarted. Major Anya Amasova was grateful to Bond for saving her life. She was also attracted to him. However, she had also sworn to avenge her KGB lover's death. Her finger tightened on the trigger…

# NAOMI

**The arrival** of Stromberg's sultry pilot affected Bond and Anya Amasova in different ways. Bond was cheerfully enthusiastic— "What a handsome craft, such lovely lines" —while Anya felt an unwelcome pang of jealousy. Anya mistrusted Naomi from the start and she was proved right. Naomi soon showed her claws.

**Aboard her helicopter,** Naomi bade Bond and Anya farewell. She had orders to kill them both. Moments later, she was blown out of the sky.

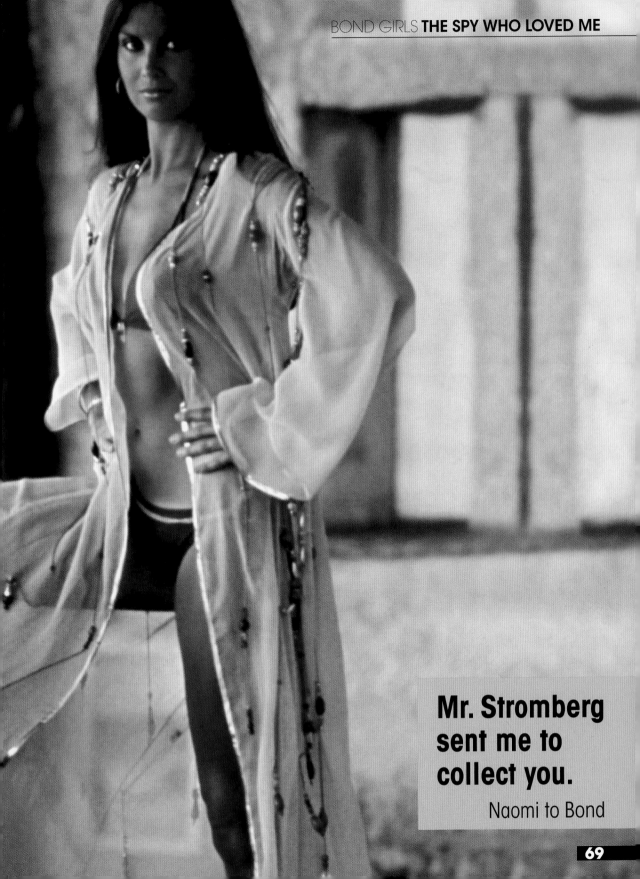

## Mr. Stromberg sent me to collect you.

Naomi to Bond

# MOONRAKER ™

**An American space shuttle** in the Royal Air Force's care
has vanished and Bond visits the shuttle's manufacturer,
Hugo Drax. Bond's reception is chilly, but the atmosphere
improves when Bond meets astronaut Dr. Holly Goodhead.
An attack on his life deepens Bond's suspicions about
Drax, and pilot Corinne Dufour helps Bond learn more
about Drax's operation—before she meets an untimely
end. In Venice, Bond discovers that Holly works for the CIA
and is also investigating Drax. After disagreements and
misunderstandings aplenty, Bond and Holly join forces to
destroy Drax's plan to use his aerospace empire to
conquer the world.

I suppose you're right. We would
be better off working together.
Détente? **Agreed.**
Understanding? **Possibly.**
Co-operation? **Maybe.**
Trust? **Out of the question.**

Bond and **Holly Goodhead**

Could this possibly be the moment for us to pool our resources?

Holly Goodhead to Bond

# DR. HOLLY GOODHEAD

**They met at Drax's** aerospace complex. Holly was an astronaut and CIA agent. She resented Bond's surprise when he discovered that "Dr. Goodhead" was a woman. Like Bond, Holly was investigating Drax, but she saw Bond as a rival, not an ally. It took time and several narrow escapes before Holly and Bond realized that, if they were going to defeat Drax, the closer they worked together, the better.

**"I still don't know** if I trust you." On Brazil's Sugarloaf Mountain, Holly discovered that Bond was the ideal man to have around in a crisis.

# CORINNE

**Drax Industries employee** and pilot Corinne Dufour was attracted to Bond and pleased when he entered her bedroom in Drax's chateau. She didn't mind that Bond also desired information and helped him to find Drax's safe. Unfortunately, their liaison was observed by Drax's henchman, Chang, and Corinne's employment was soon terminated—permanently.

My mother gave me a list of things not to do on a first date.

Corinne Dufour

# FOR YOUR EYES ONLY™

**When her parents are gunned down,** Melina Havelock does not hesitate—she pursues the killer. A bolt from her crossbow thuds into his back, enabling a captured MI6 agent, James Bond, to escape with her. Melina teams up with Bond on a secret mission to complete her parents' work: salvaging the missing ATAC defense system, lost on the Mediterranean seabed. Their search leads to brutal clashes with a gang of thugs and killers led by the duplicitous Kristatos, who plans to sell the ATAC to the KGB.

# <u>You</u> don't tell <u>me</u> what to do!

Melina Havelock to Bond

# MELINA HAVELOCK

**Half-English, half-Greek,** grief-stricken marine archaeologist Melina Havelock turned crossbow-wielding avenger. Not satisfied with killing her parents' grinning assassin, she also wanted retribution against his paymaster. Her resolve led her to team up with Bond as he battled underworld kingpin Kristatos for possession of the ATAC defense system. Only when Kristatos was dead could her thoughts turn from revenge to romance.

**Crossbow at the ready,** Melina played a full part in an attack on Kristatos's clifftop lair led by Bond.

**"For your eyes only,** darling." With the mission at an end, Melina suggested a moonlight swim.

Greek women,
like Elektra,
always avenge
their loved ones.

Melina to Bond

Whoops, me nightie's slipping.
**So is your accent, Countess.**

Countess Lisl and **Bond**

**The next morning,** as they strolled along a beach, the Countess was murdered by assassin Emile Locque. Bond soon avenged her brutal death.

# COUNTESS LISL

**She claimed** to come from Austrian nobility, but "Countess Lisl Von Schlaf" was really from Liverpool in England. She and Bond both wanted information from each other, but as the wine flowed and the hour grew late, the Countess and Bond temporarily forgot their respective missions.

# OCTOPUSSY™

**Bond's investigation** into a jewel-smuggling ring that replaces stolen Russian art treasures with fakes leads him to India and an encounter with the charismatic Octopussy. A life of crime has brought Octopussy fabulous wealth: she dwells in the Floating Palace, a private island where men are forbidden, surrounded by her own army of female guards. Bond discovers that Octopussy's chief accomplice, art dealer Kamal Khan, is in league with General Orlov, a warmongering Soviet general who plans to use Octopussy's Circus to plant an atomic bomb in a US air base in West Germany. Bond foils the plot, and he and Octopussy team up to put an end to the treacherous Khan.

So you are the mysterious Octopussy.
**And you are James Bond, Double-O-Seven, licensed to kill. Am I to be your target for tonight?**

Bond and **Octopussy**

# OCTOPUSSY'S
# GIRLS

**They came** from all over Southeast Asia, looking for a guru, seeking spiritual discipline. They found what they were looking for in Octopussy's revived Octopus cult, learning commando techniques as guards at Octopussy's Floating Palace and acrobatic skills as part of her circus troupe. Each one was chosen for her athleticism and loyalty. Octopussy's girls were a formidable fighting force, as Kamal Khan and his followers would discover.

**I train them, give them a purpose. A sisterhood and a way of life.**
In crime?
**In business.**

**Octopussy** and Bond

**I collect memories.**
Well, lets get on with making a few.

**Magda** and Bond

# MAGDA

**Cool, enigmatic,** and sinuously athletic, Magda was an important member of Octopussy's smuggling organization. She helped Kamal Khan to reclaim a precious jewel by seducing Bond and she was also the ringmaster of Octopussy's Circus. When Octopussy's army attacked Kamal Khan's palace, Magda was in the thick of the fight.

**Although** she was the ringmaster of Octopussy's Circus, Magda was unaware of Khan's bomb plot.

# A VIEW TO A KILL ™

**As soon as** Bond sees geologist Stacey Sutton arrive at Max Zorin's chateau, he senses that she could hold the key to his investigation into the microchip magnate's organization. Several attempts on his life later, Bond teams up with Stacey to foil Zorin's attempt to corner the world's microchip market. Her professional expertise helps uncover Zorin's master plan, Project Main Strike, and foil his attempt to bring about an earthquake that will destroy California's Silicon Valley and millions of innocent lives.

## I can tell you a few things about Zorin.

I'd like to hear them.

**Stacey Sutton** and Bond

## I'd sell everything and live in a tent before I'd give up.

Stacey Sutton to Bond

# STACEY SUTTON

**Zorin made a mistake** when he tried to intimidate Stacey Sutton. First, he tried to use the law to get hold of her company, Sutton Oil. Then he tried bribery, and finally he tried force. Stacey's job as California's state geologist meant that she was in a unique position to expose Zorin when he began pumping sea water into his oil wells. She was desperate to stop Zorin from causing a catastrophic earthquake. Fortunately, she had Bond to help her.

**May Day** informed Stacey that her helicopter was waiting, cutting short her conversation with Bond at Max Zorin's party.

# POLA IVANOVA

**Bond was** not the only secret agent interested in Max Zorin's affairs. Former Russian ballerina and KGB spy Pola Ivanova was also on the case. Bond and Pola were old friends and rivals. A chance meeting enabled them to rekindle both aspects of their relationship. Pola had a cassette tape detailing Zorin's plans, and Bond was determined to get it. A quick switch of tapes later, and all Pola ended up with was sweet music.

Détente can be beautiful.
**This is no time to be discussing politics.**

Pola Ivanova and **Bond**

# THE LIVING DAYLIGHTS ™

**Bond senses** that the girl in the window is no professional sniper. Bond is right: Kara Milovy is more used to handling a cello than a high-powered rifle. Ordered to shoot her, Bond deliberately misses. But why the KGB would use an amateur sniper to prevent General Georgi Koskov's defection to the West remains a mystery. Bond discovers that Kara is Koskov's girlfriend, and that Koskov's motives are as false as his charming smile.

## Whoever she was, I must have scared the living daylights out of her.

Bond to Saunders,
Head of Station V, Vienna

# KARA MILOVY

**All she wanted** was a quiet life as a cellist. Kara Milovy was drawn into an international conspiracy by her lover, KGB General Georgi Koskov. He persuaded her to pose as a KGB sniper to make his defection to the West look more realistic. Then Bond came into her life, claiming to be Georgi's friend, sent to bring her out of Czechoslovakia. Kara had to decide where her loyalties lay: with the elusive Georgi, or with Bond.

**Bond and Kara** eluded Czech patrols by tobogganing across

# LICENCE TO KILL ™

**Pilot Pam Bouvier** is on Franz Sanchez's hit list. She teams up with Bond on his mission of revenge against the merciless drug baron, responsible for mutilating Bond's friend Leiter and murdering Leiter's bride. Pam's courage and flying skills prove vital to Bond's bid to destroy Sanchez and his drugs empire.

Out of gas. I haven't heard that one in a long time.

# PAM BOUVIER

Why can't you be *my* executive secretary?

**We're south of the border. It's a man's world.**

Pam Bouvier and **Bond**

**Pam had worked** for the CIA and as an army pilot in "the toughest hellholes in South America." A superb flyer and a good shot, she knew what Bond was up against in his one-man war against Franz Sanchez. Yet her tough, professional exterior concealed a sensitive, vulnerable side. As their mission against Sanchez intensified, so did her feelings for Bond.

You'd better
find yourself
another lover.

Bond

**Lupe knew** all about Franz Sanchez's sadistic ways. She had tried to escape his clutches before. Sanchez and his men had tracked her down and cut out her lover's heart. She had been brutally treated, but her spirit remained unbroken. She saw in Bond someone strong and resourceful enough to break Sanchez's stranglehold on her life.

# LUPE LAMORA

**Freed by** Sanchez's death, Lupe was very grateful to Bond. He had to make a quick decision between Lupe Lamora and Pam Bouvier—and chose Pam.

**With the fall** of the Soviet Union, old, familiar enemies have gone, replaced by new, unfamiliar ones. Change has also come to MI6 with the arrival of a new, female, M. Bond and other members of the MI6 "old guard" believe that the new M is just a "bean-counter," but she proves to be as decisive as her predecessor. M orders Bond to investigate the Janus crime syndicate, believed to have been involved in the theft of the top-secret GoldenEye weapons system from the Severnaya Space Weapons Research Center in Siberia.

If you think for one moment I don't have the balls to send a man to die, your instincts are dead wrong. I've no compunction about sending you to your death. But I won't do it on a whim.

M to Bond

How can you be so cold?
**It's what keeps me alive.**
No. It's what keeps you alone.

Natalya Simonova and **Bond**

# NATALYA SIMONOVA

**The computer programmer** miraculously survived Janus' attempt to murder the staff at Severnaya Space Weapons Research Center. Natalya traveled to St. Petersburg to find out who was behind the massacre and became a target for Janus and the Russian KGB. She became a vital ally to Bond as he tried to stop Janus from plunging Britain into chaos. .

**Bond and Natalya** had reason to smile at the end of the GoldenEye mission. Bond was sure there was no one within 25 miles…Then they were suddenly surrounded by commandos.

# XENIA ONATOPP

**Bond had never** encountered a *femme* more *fatale*. Ex-Soviet fighter pilot and Janus's chief assassin Xenia Onatopp was a super-fit, thrill-seeking psychopath who got her kicks crushing her lovers to death with her thighs. She particularly desired that James Bond should become one of her victims. He had managed to escape her clutches once. Xenia was not going to let that happen again…

**Xenia Onatopp** intercepted Bond in Cuba as he and his partner, Natalya Simonova, searched for Janus's Cuban base. Onatopp went straight on the attack.

**No more foreplay.
Take me to Janus.**

**Bond** to Xenia Onatopp

# MONEYPENNY

**What would I ever do without you?** As far as I can remember, James, you've never had me. **Hope springs eternal**.

**Bond** and Moneypenny

**She was too professional** to mix pleasure with business. However, M's secretary, Moneypenny, enjoyed giving as good as she got whenever Bond started flirting with her. The advent of a female boss had helped to dispel the all-male "boys club" atmosphere at MI6. Moneypenny felt emboldened to tease Bond back, jokingly accusing him of "sexual harassment." When he asked her what the penalty for that was, she had her answer ready: "Someday, you have to make good on your innuendos." Moneypenny sometimes wondered if Bond ever would…

# *Tomorrow Never Dies* ™

**Bond meets Wai Lin** of the Chinese Secret Service at the launch of media mogul Elliot Carver's satellite news network. Bond poses as a banker; Wai Lin as a science journalist. They are there to investigate Carver, whom they suspect is involved in the mysterious sinking of a British warship, wildly off course in waters the Chinese believe are theirs. Has Carver's immensely powerful media empire been *creating* events rather than simply reporting them? At first in competition, later in partnership, Bond and Wai Lin take on Carver's gang of techno-terrorists and killers in order to foil his plot to provoke war between Britain and China and gain exclusive Chinese satellite transmission rights for 100 years.

# If I didn't know better, I'd say you were following me around, Mr. Bond.

Wai Lin

# WAI LIN

**Calm, efficient,** a martial artist experienced with all kinds of weapons, Wai Lin prided herself on working alone. However, she had to admit that, while handcuffed together, she and Bond had helped each other out of some deadly situations. After Bond saved her from taking a bullet, she decided to team up with him in order to destroy Carver's stealth ship and avert a war.

**As a token** of their new partnership, Wai Lin handed Bond a special earring so he could pick the lock on his handcuffs.

**Thugs hired** by Elliot Carver attacked Wai Lin at her supposedly secret Saigon hideout. She fought them off—with a little help from Bond.

**You still think you can do this alone?**

It depends whether your mission is peace or revenge.

**Bond** and Wai Lin

You know, this job of yours—
it's murder on relationships.

Paris to Bond

# PARIS CARVER

**Questioned by** her jealous husband Elliot, Paris Carver claimed to know Bond only slightly. However, a Carver spy had overheard her asking Bond: "Do you still sleep with a gun under your pillow?" In truth, Bond and Paris had once been very close—too close for Bond's comfort. The flame still burned between them. Paris was willing to help Bond with his investigation of her husband, but her life was in deadly danger.

# The World Is Not Enough™

**Elektra King**—charming, beautiful, psychotic—holds a grudge against her oil magnate father Sir Robert and M, but neither of them suspects it… Elektra was once kidnapped by the terrorist Renard. M and her father took a stand and refused to pay her ransom on principle; Elektra escaped by seducing Renard and shooting her way out… Now Elektra wants revenge. She secretly teams up with her lover, Renard, to murder her father and take over his oil business. She then plots to secure a monopoly on distribution to the West for her new pipeline by wiping Istanbul off the map. For extra satisfaction, she also plans the deaths of M and Bond, whom she blames for using her as bait to catch Renard.

**I'm going to redraw the map. And when I'm through, the whole world will know my name.**

Elektra King to Bond

# ELEKTRA KING

**She had toyed** with Bond, but it was Renard she loved—not so much for himself, but for what he could do for her. As a lover, Renard was useless: a bullet from an MI6 agent's gun was in his brain, robbing him of any ability to feel and slowly killing him. Elektra would have preferred Bond, but he was wedded to his duty. That made Elektra hate him.

**There's no point in living
if you can't feel alive.**

Elektra King

# CHRISTMAS JONES

**In the male-dominated field** of nuclear physics, Dr. Christmas Jones was used to standing up for herself. Christmas first encountered Bond at a former Soviet test site in Kazakhstan, where she was decommissioning atomic devices. Renard's theft of nuclear material brought her and Bond together in a desperate bid to prevent Renard from blowing up the city of Istanbul.

**Miss—?**

Doctor. Jones. Christmas Jones. And don't make any jokes, I've heard them all.

**Bond** and Christmas Jones

**Christmas** helped Bond to surprise gangster Valentin Zukovsky at his caviar factory. Zukovsky confessed that he had supplied Elektra King with a decommissioned Russian nuclear submarine.

# DIE ANOTHER DAY ™

**Jinx and Bond** are two of a kind—committed to their respective intelligence agencies, determined to see a mission through to the bitter end, seizing the moment when it comes to love. They meet in Cuba, both on the trail of a terrorist named Zao, who is undergoing an illegal gene therapy program to change his appearance. They renew their acquaintance in Iceland, investigating diamond magnate Gustav Graves and his Icarus space mirror. The two agents make a powerful team as they battle Graves's attempt to use Icarus as a weapon to destroy South Korea and create a single Korean superpower.

**Do you believe in bad luck?**
Let's just say my relationships don't seem to last.
**Hmm. I know the feeling.**

**Bond** and Jinx

> **I'm a girl who just doesn't like to get tied down.**
>
> Jinx to Bond

# JINX

**Whatever Jinx did,** she did in style. She showed up at Graves's Ice Palace driving a sleek Ford Thunderbird. For the party celebrating the launch of Graves's Icarus space mirror, she changed into a spectacular Versace dress. Bond was doubly impressed—he already knew what a devastatingly effective agent Jinx was.

**Posing as Miss Swift** from *Space and Technology Magazine*, Jinx cut a dash in a tight leather outfit as she arrived at Graves's Ice Palace.

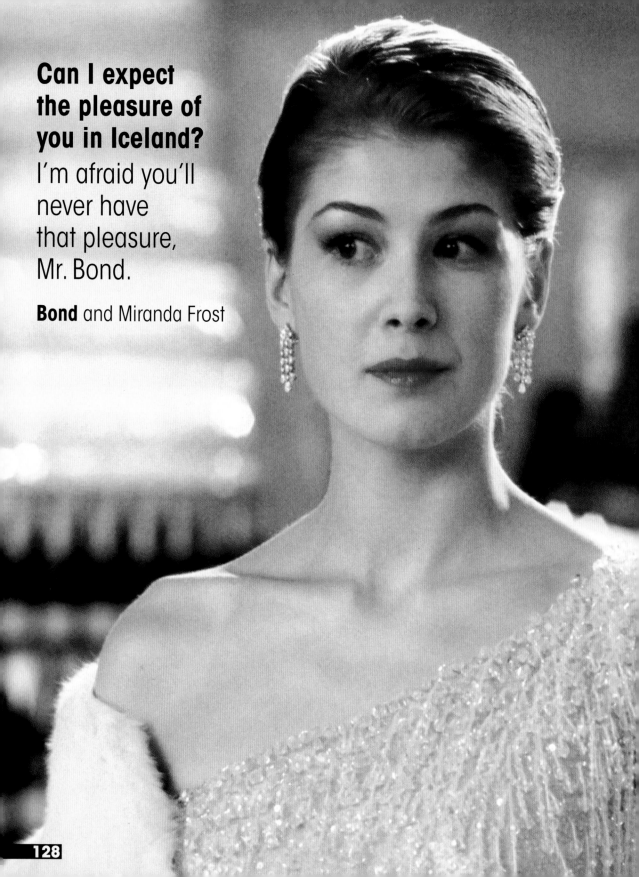

**Can I expect the pleasure of you in Iceland?**

I'm afraid you'll never have that pleasure, Mr. Bond.

**Bond** and Miranda Frost

# MIRANDA FROST

**Champion fencer** Miranda Frost had cheated her way to an Olympic gold medal and she deceived both M and Bond. They believed she was spying on Gustav Graves for MI6. However, she was in league with the diamond magnate and shared his power-crazed dreams. Miranda's icy hauteur intrigued and attracted Bond, but he couldn't melt Miranda's heart. She developed a particular hatred for Bond's female partner, NSA agent Jinx.

**Miranda Frost** surprised Jinx on board Graves's flying command center. A battle to the death with swords and knives ensued, and Ms. Frost met her match at last.

**129**

# CASINO ROYALE

**M believes** that MI6's newest double-O agent, James Bond, is reckless, arrogant, and emotionally detached. Her assessment is spot-on—until Bond meets and falls in love with Vesper Lynd. Vesper introduces herself to Bond as "the money," the Treasury agent responsible for staking Bond in his bid to defeat banker-to-terrorists Le Chiffre at poker and bring him in for interrogation. The violent twists and turns of the assignment bring Bond and Vesper closer and closer together. Bond even promises to leave MI6 for her. Then he discovers that she was working for the enemy all along.

**You aren't going to let me in there, are you? You've got your armor back on and that's that.**

I have no armor left. You stripped it off me and tossed it away.

**Vesper Lynd** and Bond

**Does everyone have a tell?**
Everyone but you. I wonder if that's
why I love you. The enigma thing.

**Vesper** and Bond

# VESPER LYND

**Their love affair** began with a form of psychoanalytical poker, which Vesper won hands down. Bond observed that Vesper's problem was her beauty, which made her professionally insecure. Vesper countered by saying that Bond had a chip on his shoulder about his orphan background and treated women as "disposable pleasures." Bond left their first meeting feeling as skewered as the lamb he had just eaten.

**For a few,** all-too-brief weeks with Bond, Vesper almost believed she could escape the evil organization that had taken over her life.

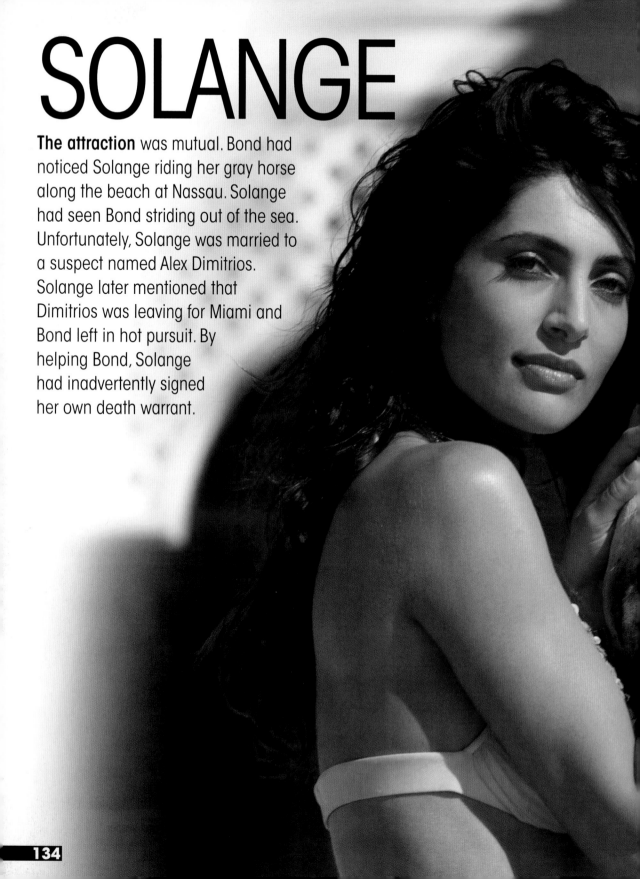

# SOLANGE

**The attraction** was mutual. Bond had
noticed Solange riding her gray horse
along the beach at Nassau. Solange
had seen Bond striding out of the sea.
Unfortunately, Solange was married to
a suspect named Alex Dimitrios.
Solange later mentioned that
Dimitrios was leaving for Miami and
Bond left in hot pursuit. By
helping Bond, Solange
had inadvertently signed
her own death warrant.

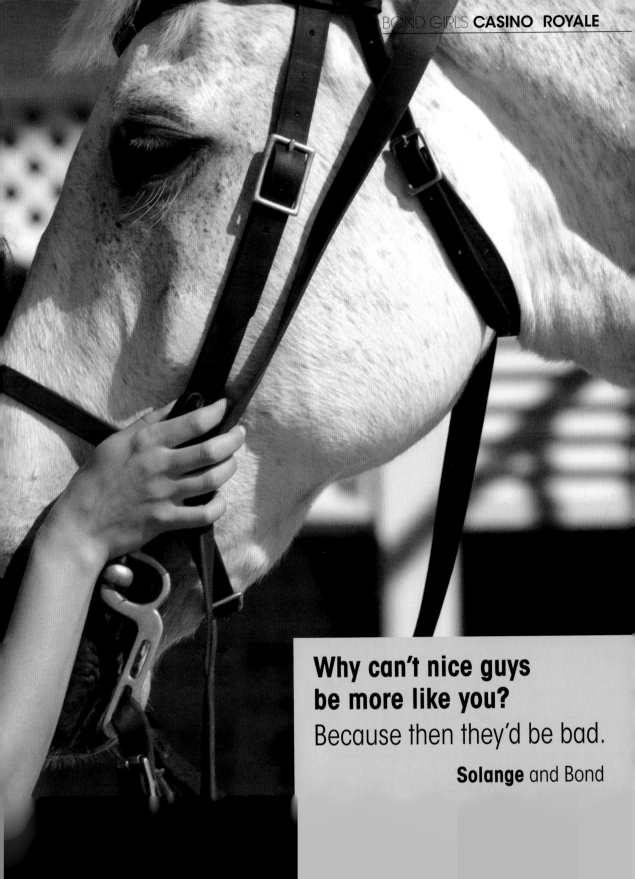

**Why can't nice guys be more like you?**
Because then they'd be bad.

**Solange** and Bond

# QUANTUM OF SOLACE

**Bond is determined** to get revenge on Quantum, the insidious organization that destroyed Vesper. Bond's vendetta angers M, but Bond finds a kindred spirit in Camille Montes. She is playing a dangerous game—cozying up to Quantum's Dominic Greene in order to get at the man who murdered her family, General Medrano.

You lost somebody? **I did, yes.**
You catch whoever did it? **No, not yet.**
Tell me when you do. I'd like to know how it feels

# CAMILLE

**There is something horribly efficient about you.**

Camille to Bond

**Her back bore** the scars from the fire—the fire started by General Medrano to cover up the murders of her parents and elder sister. A fire also raged within Camille Montes to be avenged against this would-be Bolivian dictator. Camille had become Dominic Greene's lover in order to assassinate Medrano. Greene tried to have Camille killed, and so she joined Bond's crusade against Greene and Quantum. Medrano's death remained Camille's priority; revenge for Vesper's death was Bond's. Camille and Bond had no time to spare for romance.

**Camille froze** in terror as fire tore through Medrano's hotel room. Bond's quick-thinking saved both of their lives.

# AGENT FIELDS

**The order** to put Bond on the first plane back to London was clear, but Bond's charisma won Agent Fields over. Almost before she knew it, he was whisking her off to a luxury hotel for the night and she had become his willing accomplice against Quantum's Dominic Greene. Fields would pay a terrible price for siding with Bond.

**Greene vented** his anger at Bond by attacking a far more vulnerable target. Bond returned to his hotel to find that Agent Fields had been drowned in crude oil.

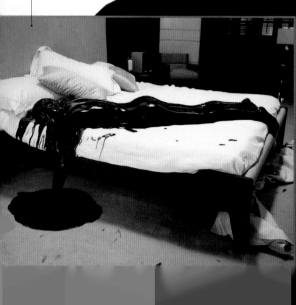

James Bond will return…

**Senior Editor** Alastair Dougall
**Senior Designer** Mark Richards
**Managing Editor** Catherine Saunders
**Art Director** Lisa Lanzarini
**Publishing Manager** Simon Beecroft
**Category Publisher** Alex Allan
**Production Editor** Siu Yin Chan
**Production Controller** Nick Seston
**US Editor** Anne Marie Ryan

First published in the United States in 2010 by DK Publishing,
375 Hudson Street, New York, New York 10014

10 11 12 13 14  10 9 8 7 6 5 4 3 2 1
177926 – 05/10

DK books are available at special discounts when purchased in bulk for sales
promotions, premiums, fund-raising, or educational use. For details, contact:
DK Publishing Special Markets, 375 Hudson Street, New York, New York 10014  or
SpecialSales@dk.com

A catalog record for this book is available from the Library of Congress.

ISBN: 978-0-7566-6874-7

Scanning and retouching by MDP, UK
Color proofing by Alta Image, UK
Printed and bound in China by Leo Paper Products Ltd

**Discover more at www.dk.com**

The author and publisher would like to thank Jenni McMurrie of EON Productions for
her invaluable help during the production of this book.